# HIDDEN PICTURES
# COLORING BOOK

## *Zoo*

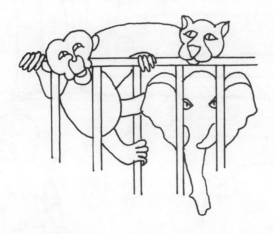

*illustrated by Tanya Maiboroda*

14 13 12 11 10 9 8

Copyright © 1987 By Tanya Maiboroda and RGA Publishing Group, Inc.
Published by Price Stern Sloan, Inc.
11150 Olympic Boulevard, Suite 650, Los Angeles, California 90064

Printed in the United States of America. All rights reserved. No part of this publication may be reproduced, stored in a retrieval system or transmitted, in any form or by any means, electronic, mechanical, photocopying, recording or otherwise, without the prior written permission of the publishers.

ISBN 0-8431-1879-2

## PRICE STERN SLOAN
Los Angeles

**Find the three gazelles.**

**Find the word "zoo" five times.**

**Find the seven snakes.**

**Find the four monkeys.**

**Find the three llamas.**

**Find the three zebras.**

**Find the two foxes.**

**Find the two armadillos.**

**Find the three tortoises.**

**Find the three koalas.**

**Find the four fish.**

**Find the two sloths.**

**Find the two squirrels.**

**Find the four rabbits.**

**Find the thirteen birds.**

**Find the four mice.**

**Find the four lizards.**

**Find the four pandas.**

**Find the six ladybugs.**

**Find the three giraffes.**

**Find the two hippos.**

**Find the two hot dogs, one hamburger and
one ice cream cone.**

**Find the four boxes of popcorn.**

**Find the six sheep.**

**Find the five bananas.**

**Find the eight ducks.**

**Find the four rhinoceroses.**

**Find the four children.**

**Find the five cats.**

**Find the four bears.**

**Find the three tigers.**

**Find the four seals.**

**Find the four elephants.**

**Find the five alligators.**

**Find the three camels.**

**Find the two porcupines.**

**Find the two anteaters.**

**Find the three beavers.**

**Find the three kangaroos.**

**Find the three raccoons.**

**Find the one reindeer.**

**Find the one bird, one butterfly, one bear, one rabbit and one cat.**

**Find the one elephant, one bird,
one bear and one snake.**

**Find the one rhinoceros, one zebra, one giraffe, one bear, one snake and one lion.**

**Find the two birds, one panda, one elephant, one lion, one snake, one monkey and one giraffe.**